Halle and the Hammer

RICHARD O'NEILL
AND MICHELLE RUSSELL

ILLUSTRATED BY ELIJAH VARDO

BLOOMSBURY EDUCATION

LONDON   OXFORD   NEW YORK   NEW DELHI   SYDNEY

BLOOMSBURY EDUCATION
Bloomsbury Publishing Plc
50 Bedford Square, London, WC1B 3DP, UK
29 Earlsfort Terrace, Dublin 2, Ireland

BLOOMSBURY, BLOOMSBURY EDUCATION and the Diana logo
are trademarks of Bloomsbury Publishing Plc

First published in Great Britain in 2023 by Bloomsbury Publishing Plc

A catalogue record for this book is available from the British Library

ISBN: PB: 978-1-80199-045-5; ePDF: 978-1-80199-042-4; ePub: 978-1-80199-046-2;
Enhanced ePub: 978-1-80199-044-8

2 4 6 8 10 9 7 5 3 1

Text design by Sarah Malley

Printed and bound in China by Leo Paper Products, Heshan, Guangdong

To find out more about our authors and books visit www.bloomsbury.com
and sign up for our newsletters

Chapter One

Halle, just like Mum, Dad and Grandma, was good at fixing and making things.

Her little brother Henry also liked to help, but he could get himself into a right mess. Which sometimes made Halle sigh but often made her laugh.

our family

Luckily, Grandma was always nearby to make sure Halle and Henry kept themselves safe. Grandma would say, "Now, that's an interesting pickle you've got yourself into."

Grandma and Henry would then chat about how he could get out of the pickle.

Halle loved listening to their plans and Henry's smile always beamed brightly when the plan worked.

It was important to learn from the mistakes they made but helping each other when things were difficult was important too. Interesting things often happened when they helped others.

This is exactly what the family were
going to do. They were on a mission
to help the people who lived in the
village of Trindle.
The last time they had visited Trindle
there had been a running race
taking place.

Mum had parked their truck near the village green. Dad had set up some chairs and they'd sat and waited with all the other people for the runners to arrive. They had been excited to see who would win and get the prize.

So they had waited… and waited… and
waited… but no runners had arrived.
While they waited, Grandma had
made everyone a nice cup of tea.
Two cups of tea later and still no
runners in sight, Mum, Dad and
the rest of the puzzled spectators
wondered what had happened.

It turned out,
not only had the wind
blown down the plastic signs
but all the runners had gone
the wrong way, following a
sign that had landed in the
branches of a tree.

Unfortunately, that sign had led the runners to a field. A field that had lost its sign, which should have said: **BEWARE OF THE BULL**.

Chapter Two

This year, Halle and her family had the important job of making some strong wooden signs that wouldn't blow over.

Just like last time, they would be taking their home with them to the village of Trindle.

The family lived together in an unusual home; one that moved from place to place. It had been specially built by Mum and Dad. The big van used to be a furniture removal truck. It was perfect for everything: sleeping, reading, drawing, cooking and, most importantly, making.

The best part was that it could be moved to wherever their customers were. Grandma, Mum and Dad always shared the driving, so sometimes Halle and Henry would go to sleep in one part of the country and wake up in another.

As well as having the usual bedrooms, kitchen and bathroom, the truck also had their workshop. This was Halle's favourite place. Just like in the living quarters, everything in the workshop had its place.

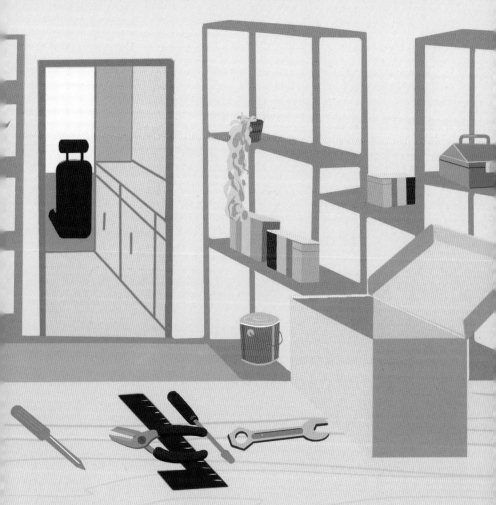

"Always put it back where it belongs," was something everyone had said to Halle when she was little and tidying her toys. The tools were no different. It was really important when they were busy making the different things that each customer needed.

Everyone needed to know where to find the right tool for the job. Halle loved how each tool had a different purpose and she had learned how to use the tools when she was very small. Now it was her turn to teach Henry.

Yesterday, Halle had shown him how to use a piece of cardboard to hold a nail in place while you tapped it in.

It hadn't taken long for Henry to work out how hard to hit the nail.

That meant he could now hold the nail between his finger and thumb, without hitting them.

When they had finished, Halle reminded Henry to tidy all the tools away – she would be needing her hammer for their important job in Trindle.

Dad was very impressed with the box they had made – it was perfect for stopping Henry's toy cars from rolling off the shelf. Mum thought it might also come in useful for keeping their books from falling over too.

Chapter Three

After parking the truck by the village hall, Dad lowered the ramp and unlocked the door to reveal the place where long pieces of wood could be stored. They'd been really lucky.

The last job at the old farm had lots of waste wood that could be recycled.

The local school had also been busy collecting other useful pieces of timber for them to use.

The rest of the family sprang into action with their well-practised routine. First things first – pull out the canopy from the side of the truck. It acted like a gazebo where they could sit and eat and work, whether it was hot sun or heavy rain.

Next – have a nice cup of tea or a cool drink of water and something tasty to eat. Tummies full and thirsts quenched, Grandma and Henry checked the map and set off to find all the places where the signs would go.

They were going to report back whether each sign needed to be fixed to a post in the ground or if it could be fixed to something else.

As they cycled away, Mum, Dad and Halle set up the workbench and found the tools that they needed.

This was Halle's favourite part as she had her own set of tools and a tool box that was her most treasured possession.

To begin with, Halle's toolbox had been empty. As she mastered how to use each tool, she had been given one of her own.

She had built up quite a collection. Halle thought she might need her hammer so she opened the lid of the tool box and lifted out the tray that was home to one pencil, two screwdrivers and three boxes labelled "nuts & bolts", "nails" and "screws".

Placing the tray on the ground she peered into the box. Spirit level... tape measure... mallet... scissors... wrench... a folded piece of paper... but no hammer! Halle unfolded the piece of paper to reveal a picture with Henry's name written in small letters in the corner.

Oh no! Henry had been the last person to use the hammer.

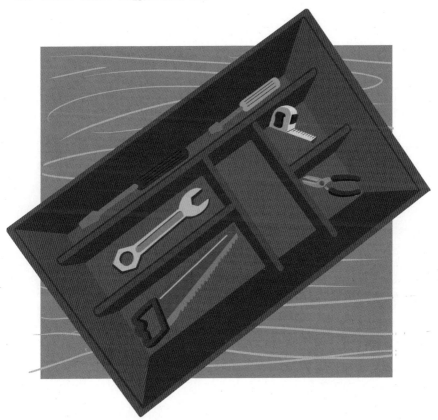

She checked the toolbox again: one pencil, two screwdrivers, three boxes, a spirit level, a tape measure, a mallet, a pair of scissors, a wrench, no hammer!

"Don't worry, love. I'm sure Henry will be able to help you find it when he gets back," said Mum.

Chapter Four

While she waited for Henry, Halle helped Mum and Dad organise the recycled timber they'd got for the signs. They looked at the designs Mum had drawn – she'd put measurements on too.

Time to measure the timber, not once but twice. Dad always used the old saying, "Measure twice, cut once". They used a metal angle rule to make sure that the signs had the right kind of point.

Then it was time to cut with the saw.
Halle was very careful.

She made sure that the wood she was
sawing was firmly held in the jaws
of a woodworking vice as she cut her
first angle.

By the time Grandma and Henry returned, all of the signs were cut and Halle hadn't needed her hammer once. But she was still worried about it. "Henry, where have you put my hammer?" said Halle.

"Oh, I can't remember," said Henry.
"I left you a map so you'd know, though."
Halle realised that Henry's picture was
like a treasure map.
She didn't think it was very useful;
everywhere she looked there was no
hammer to be found.

The search for the missing hammer was interrupted by her rumbling tummy. After lunch, Henry opened the box they had made which had his cars safe inside. To Halle's surprise, her hammer was there too!

She was so pleased to find it that she quickly forgot that Henry's map had not been very helpful. She carefully put her hammer back in her toolbox.

Chapter Five

The whole family set to sanding the signs, making sure that they were smooth and ready to be painted. Grandma was the best at painting. Henry kept her supplied with all the right colours and paintbrushes. One by one, the pointy pieces of wood became signs.

When the signs were all laid out with the paint drying, the family had a well-earned rest.

That evening they met up with some children and their teacher from the village school. Everyone was very excited to see the new signs.

"What do they look like?" the
teacher asked.
"Like nothing you've ever seen before,"
Grandma replied.
"Very bright," said Halle.
"Beautiful," said Mum.
"I helped with the paint brushes,"
said Henry.

"Look – here they are," said Dad.
The signs didn't disappoint. They were
everything the family had described.
Halle listened as the plans were made
to move the signs to their new homes.
Henry was very proud as Grandma
shared a second map he had made,
marking each location.

Chapter Six

The next morning, the signs were loaded into a farmer's trailer, and delivered to the places that were marked on Henry's map.

Halle and Henry set down their fold-out chairs and waited with all the other people for the runners to arrive.

The school children waved their flags as their teacher looked towards the path where one of the signs had been fixed in place. They couldn't wait to see who would be the winner and get the prize.

They waited… and waited… and waited… Halle began to wonder if following Henry's map had been such a good idea.

They waited…

    and waited…

        and waited…

Then, quick as a flash, the first runner who was wearing a red top passed by, closely followed by a second in yellow. They darted towards the finish line but were both pipped at the post by a runner in green. Everyone cheered.

The race this year was a huge success. The villagers decided that Henry's map was so helpful that it could be used like a treasure trail for visitors to find the signs.

The next day, as they finished packing up the van, Dad told Halle and Henry that they would be back next year to help the school children learn how to use their own tools to make something useful.

Clunk. Click! Halle and Henry buckled up. The family, all packed up and excited to go, headed off, ready to help make and fix things for new people in new places.

BEEP!
BEEP!